AARON BLABEY

the DREADFUL FLUFF

CALGARY PUBLIC LIBRARY

APR - 2018

PUFFIN BOOKS

For the boy who changed everything.

PUFFIN BOOKS

UK | USA | Canada | Ireland | Australia
India | New Zealand | South Africa | China

Penguin Books is part of the Penguin Random House group of companies
whose addresses can be found at global.penguinrandomhouse.com

Published by Penguin Group (Australia), 2012
This paperback edition published by Penguin Group (Australia), 2016
This edition published by Penguin Random House Pty Ltd, 2017

Text and illustration copyright © Aaron Blabey, 2012

The moral right of the author has been asserted.

Cover and text design by Aaron Blabey and Elissa Webb © Penguin Group (Australia)
Printed and bound in China

Cataloguing-in-Publication data is available from the National Library of Australia

ISBN: 978 0 14 350700 0

penguin.com.au

Serenity Strainer was perfect.

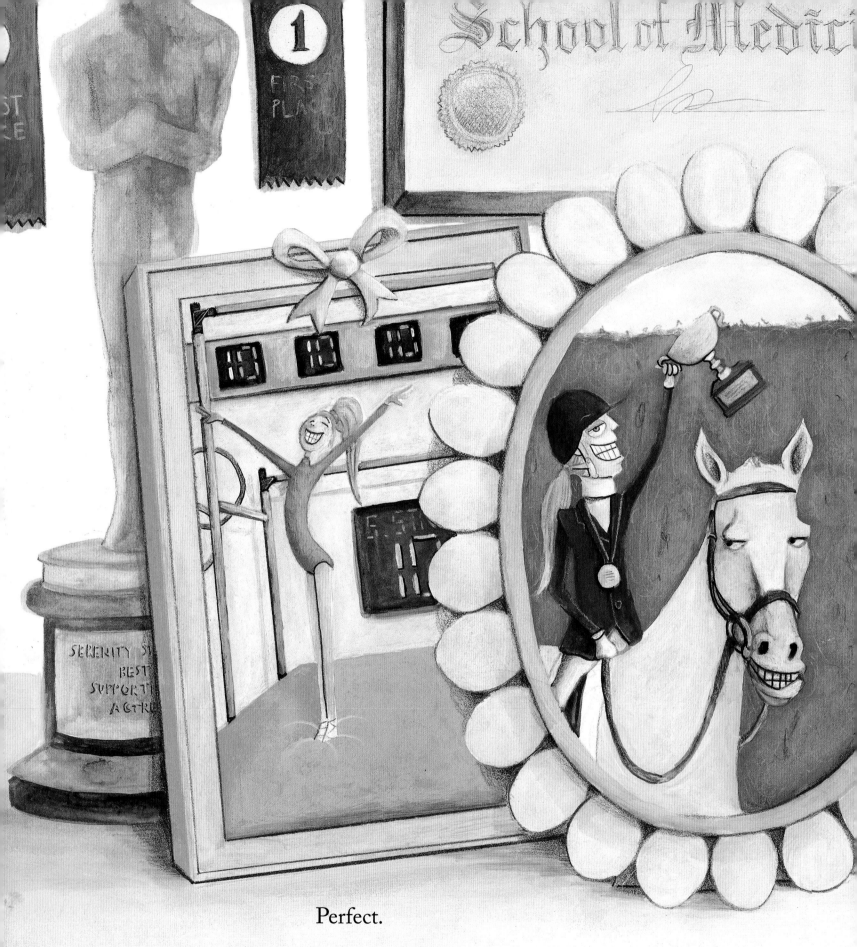

Perfect.

Perfect.

Perfect.

Perfect.

But one Saturday morning,
she discovered something perfectly *awful*.

'BELLY BUTTON FLUFF!?
That can't possibly be mine!' she said.

But it was.

And guess what?

It was evil.

The Dreadful Fluff said something so rude that Serenity went weak at the knees.

Then it farted and tore off across the bathroom floor.

At incredible speed, it sprang into the pocket of Serenity's perfectly stylish coat . . .

. . . and when it popped back up, all covered in lint, it was a good deal bigger than it was before.

'YOU GHASTLY THING!' she said.

But the Dreadful Fluff just coughed up something nasty and rolled off down the hall.

By the time it reached
the end of the perfectly
fabulous shag pile rug,
it was even bigger
than the cat.

And, I'm sorry to say, it ate him.

Then it hurtled into the laundry and set about making itself even bigger.

Unfortunately, Serenity's mother was doing a load of washing at the time.

Poor Mrs Strainer never stood a chance.

'GIVE ME BACK MY MUM!' cried Serenity.

But something had already
caught the Dreadful Fluff's eye.

'Oh no,' said Serenity Strainer.

The Dreadful Fluff plunged under Tug Strainer's bed and came out the other side roughly the size of a Shetland pony.

Serenity's big brother never knew what hit him.

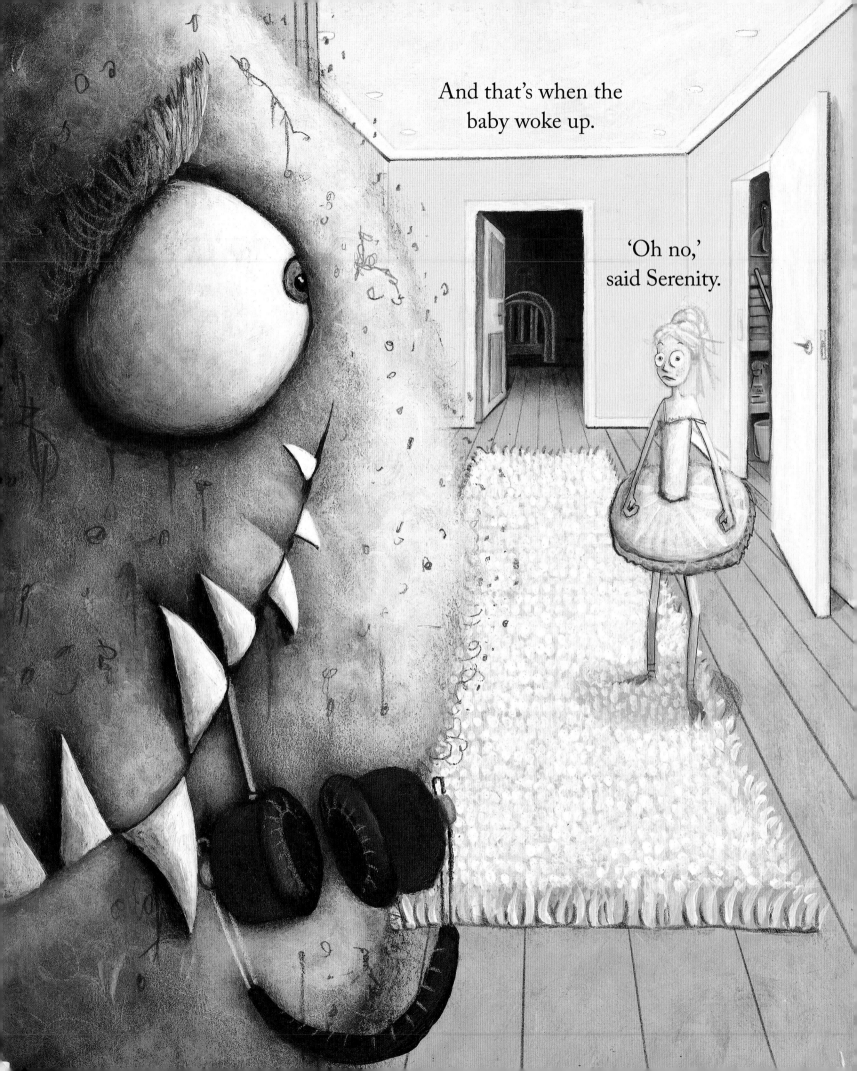

And that's when the baby woke up.

'Oh no,' said Serenity.

She tried her best to block its way...

but the Dreadful Fluff just brushed her aside ...

and squeezed itself through the nursery door.

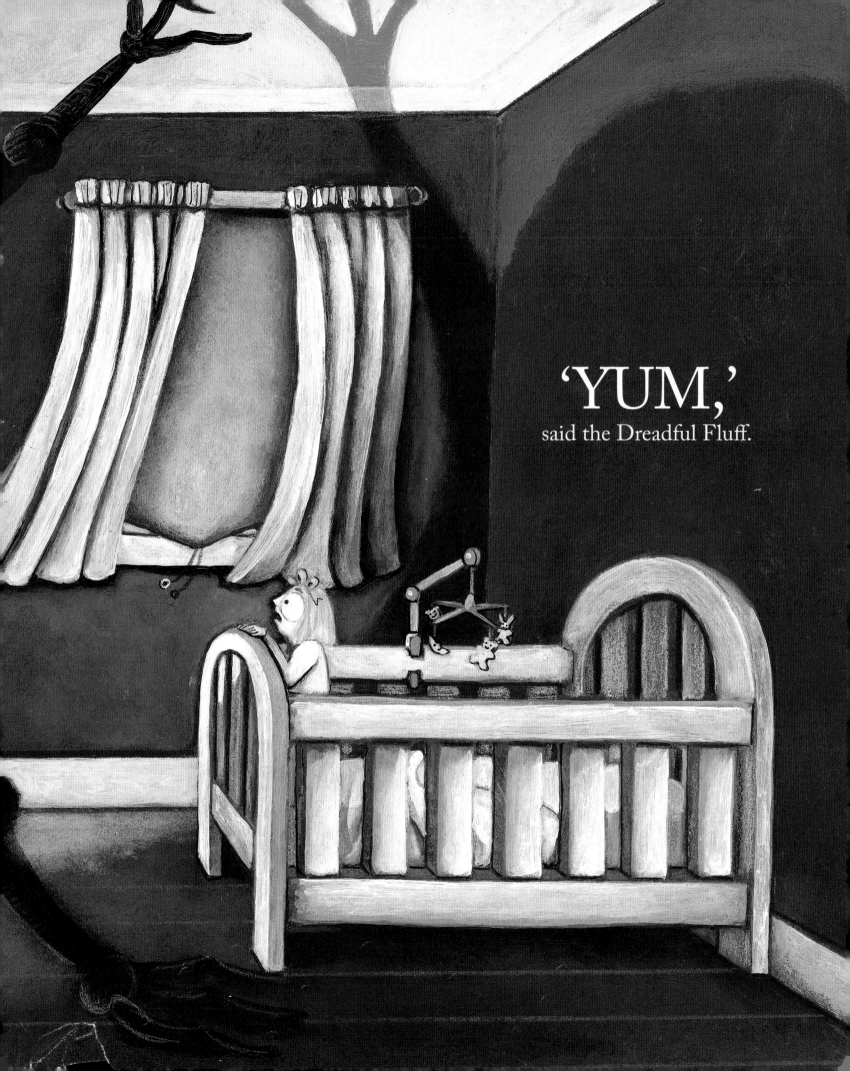

'YUM,'
said the Dreadful Fluff.

'I don't think so,'
said Serenity Strainer.

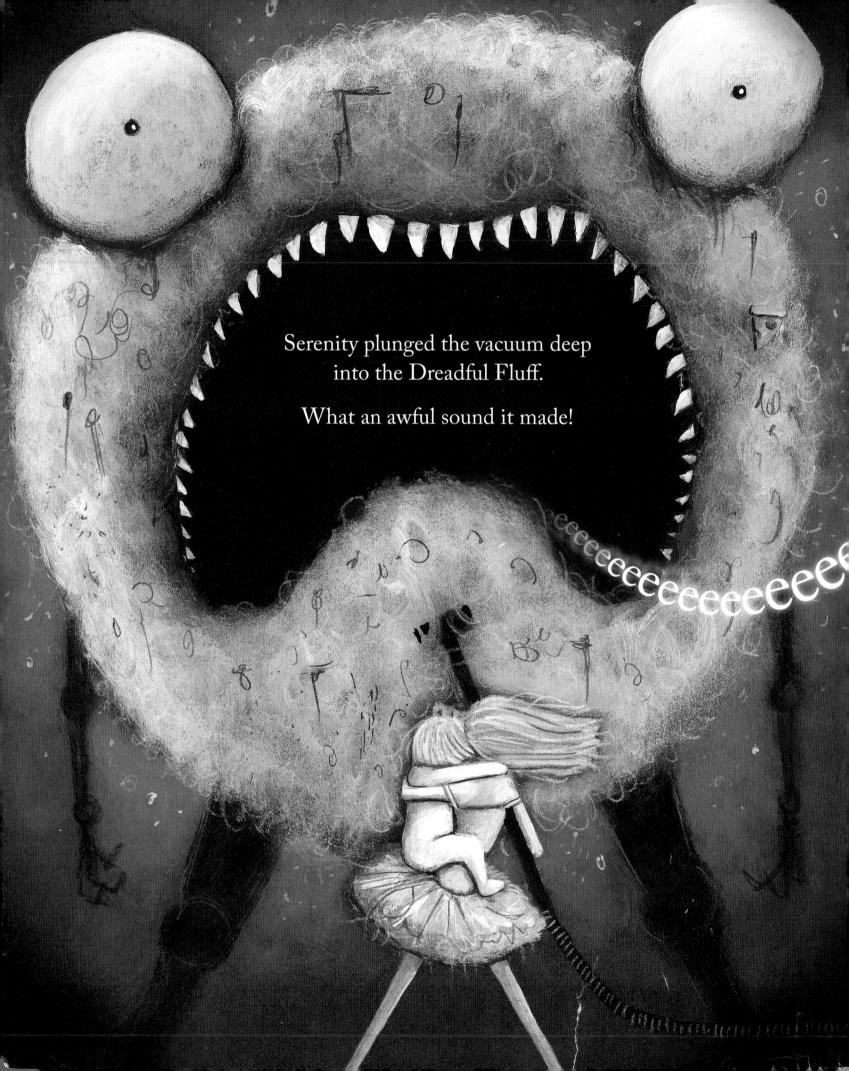

Serenity plunged the vacuum deep
into the Dreadful Fluff.

What an awful sound it made!

And then, with a *pop*!

And a *splat*!

And the *plop* of a cat.

That was that.

For the Strainer family,
life has never really been the same again.

And Serenity?

Well, she isn't perfect.

Far from it.

But can she deal with that?

She can deal with it perfectly well.